Dear Parents:

Congratulations! Your child is taking the first steps on an exciting journey. The destination? Independent reading!

STEP INTO READING® will help your child get there. The program offers five steps to reading success. Each step includes fun stories and colorful art or photographs. In addition to original fiction and books with favorite characters, there are Step into Reading Non-Fiction Readers, Phonics Readers and Boxed Sets, Sticker Readers, and Comic Readers—a complete literacy program with something to interest every child.

Learning to Read, Step by Step!

Ready to Read   Preschool–Kindergarten
• big type and easy words • rhyme and rhythm • picture clues
For children who know the alphabet and are eager to begin reading.

Reading with Help   Preschool–Grade 1
• basic vocabulary • short sentences • simple stories
For children who recognize familiar words and sound out new words with help.

Reading on Your Own   Grades 1–3
• engaging characters • easy-to-follow plots • popular topics
For children who are ready to read on their own.

Reading Paragraphs   Grades 2–3
• challenging vocabulary • short paragraphs • exciting stories
For newly independent readers who read simple sentences with confidence.

Ready for Chapters   Grades 2–4
• chapters • longer paragraphs • full-color art
For children who want to take the plunge into chapter books but still like colorful pictures.

STEP INTO READING® is designed to give every child a successful reading experience. The grade levels are only guides; children will progress through the steps at their own speed, developing confidence in their reading. The F&P Text Level on the back cover serves as another tool to help you choose the right book for your child.

Remember, a lifetime love of reading starts with a single step!

For Tracey Kyle,
dedicated teacher
—C.R.

Text copyright © 2022 by Candice Ransom
Cover art and interior illustrations copyright © 2022 by Ashley Evans

All rights reserved. Published in the United States by Random House Children's Books, a division of Penguin Random House LLC, New York.

Step into Reading, Random House, and the Random House colophon are registered trademarks of Penguin Random House LLC.

Visit us on the Web!
StepIntoReading.com
rhcbooks.com

Educators and librarians, for a variety of teaching tools, visit us at RHTeachersLibrarians.com

Library of Congress Cataloging-in-Publication Data is available upon request.
ISBN 978-0-593-30260-6 (trade) — ISBN 978-0-593-30261-3 (lib. bdg.) —
ISBN 978-0-593-30262-0 (ebook)

Printed in the United States of America
10 9 8 7 6 5 4 3 2 1
First Edition

This book has been officially leveled by using the F&P Text Level Gradient™ Leveling System.

STEP INTO READING®

School Day!

by Candice Ransom
illustrated by Ashley Evans

Random House 🏠 New York

Goodbye, picnics.
Goodbye, pool.

Goodbye, summer.

Hello, school!

Slip on backpacks.

Both of us.

Run to catch the
yellow bus.

Here is your room.

Meet Ms. Ball!

My room is just

up the hall.

Smiling classmates
wait for you.

Listen, learn,
and have fun, too.

Busy morning.

Spelling chart.

Little brother making art.

14

Outside

I race

down the track.

Little brother
eats his snack.

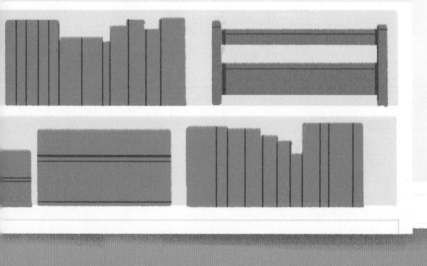

After lunch

I drop my tray.

See my brother
laugh and play.

Reading.

Writing.

Draw a map.

Lucky brother
takes a nap.

Water flowers.

Pitcher drips.

Brother waves,
then off he skips.

First day over.

Last bell rings.

Where is my brother?

Where are his things?

Check the lunchroom.

Check the playground.

Check the bus line.

Brother found!

"Look what I made.

Just for you!"

A big red heart.

"Love you, too!"